Amelia Bedelia & FRIENDS

The Cat's Meow

Daisy

me!

Holly

Joy

Clay

ip

Rose

Wade

Cliff

Penny
Angel

Heather

Dawn

Amelia Bedelia

& FRIENDS

The Cat's Meow

me

by Herman Parish

pictures by Lynne Avril

Greenwillow Books
An Imprint of HarperCollins Publishers

Library of Congress Control Number: 2019944438

ISBN 9780062935229 (hardback) — ISBN 9780062961822 (paper-over-board) —
ISBN 9780062935212 (paperback)

19 20 21 22 23 PC/LSCC 10 9 8 7 6 5 4 3 2 1 First Edition

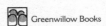
Greenwillow Books

For Eva, our cat's meow

—H. P.

This book is for Amelia Bedelia's dad,
who saved the day!

—L. A.

Contents

Chapter 1

If at First
You Don't Succeed

"Remember, people!" said Ms. Garcia, Amelia Bedelia's science teacher at Oak Tree Elementary. "All great inventors think outside the box!"

Amelia Bedelia looked at her friend Joy and shrugged. Teachers were always telling them to think outside the box. Amelia Bedelia rarely stood

1

in a box to think, and neither did any of her friends. But Amelia Bedelia had also never invented anything famous— at least not yet. Not a lightbulb, like Thomas Edison . . . or shampoo made out of peanuts, like George Washington Carver . . . or a chocolate chip cookie, like Ruth Wakefield . . . or even a pair of earmuffs, like Chester Greenwood.

Thomas Edison

Ruth Wakefield

George Washington Carver

Chester Greenwood

"An inventor starts with a problem and then finds a solution that doesn't already exist," Ms. Garcia continued. "So let's think about that for a minute. What is a problem that you

2

would like to solve?"

Amelia Bedelia's friend
Cliff waved his hand. "Too
much homework!" he shouted.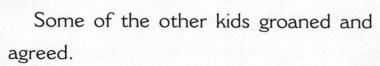

Some of the other kids groaned and
agreed.

"Okay, so what could you invent to
help with that?" asked Ms. Garcia.

"A machine that does my homework
for me?" Cliff suggested.

"Fun! But would that solve the
whole problem?" Ms. Garcia asked.
"You wouldn't have to spend so much
time doing homework, true . . . but you
also wouldn't learn anything and then
you'd be stuck at Oak Tree Elementary
forever."

"Like our big oak tree out front," said Penny.

"Can someone come up with an invention to help Cliff out?" asked Ms. Garcia.

Joy had an idea. "How about a helmet that beams homework directly from your head onto the paper? Then you'd still learn stuff, but you wouldn't spend so much time writing everything down. You could do your homework while you were having fun or even when you're asleep!"

"Excellent idea!" said Ms. Garcia. "Anybody else have a problem they'd like us to solve with an invention?"

"I hate lima beans!" said Penny called

4

out. "And my mom makes me eat them."

"Oh, a lot of people have that problem. What's your invention?" asked Ms. Garcia.

Penny drummed her fingers on her desk. "A special ring that converts lima beans into chocolate!" she said. "You could use it right at the table."

"Fantastic! Amelia Bedelia, what about you? Do you have a problem you'd like to solve?" said Ms. Garcia.

Amelia Bedelia thought about this.

Mostly she figured that her life was pretty good. Sure, some days she would rather stay home and bake than go to school . . . but then she thought about how much fun it was to see her friends. Some days her mother did indeed serve lima beans for dinner . . . but she usually made Amelia Bedelia eat only a bite or two.

But there *was* one thing. . . .

"My dog, Finally, poops in our backyard," she said. "It's my job to pick it up. And it's gross!"

The class laughed. Amelia Bedelia laughed too. It was funny . . . but it was also true! She knew it was part of taking care of a dog. She loved Finally. She loved all animals.

"Most pet owners have that same problem," Ms. Garcia said. "What's a solution?"

The class came up with a lot of ideas for this one.

A robot pooper scooper!

A spray that instantly melted poop into fertilizer!

A dog trainer who could train Finally to pick up her own poop!

Puppy diapers!

A puppy porta-potty!

"That's thinking outside the box!" said Ms. Garcia. "Very creative. Very inventive! Now, for the rest of the period, I'd like you each to try inventing something of your own."

She waved her hand toward the back of the science classroom. Piled on top of a long table were all sorts of supplies— rubber wheels, metal cogs, plastic tubes, boards with holes in them, wires, cords,

tape, glue, staples, and more.

"Here's the problem I want you to solve, inventors," she said. "Suppose you have five marbles, and you want to move all five of them at least twelve inches. You can't touch the marbles or pick them up in your hands. How can you do it? What can you make to help you? Go ahead and get started—and remember, a good inventor is nimble! You must think on your feet!"

Amelia Bedelia jumped up

from her chair and bounced up and down on her toes.

"Good inventors are persistent! They never give up!" Ms. Garcia went on. "And most importantly, a good inventor knows that there's more than one way to skin a cat. We have about thirty more minutes. Let's see who can solve it."

Amelia Bedelia froze. What a horrible idea! Who would want to skin a cat?

She looked around the classroom. There was Hermione, the corn snake, dozing in her cage, draped over a log. There was Harriet, the hamster, running happily on

her wheel, which squeaked and creaked under her tiny pink feet. No cat, which was a relief.

Amelia Bedelia and her friends headed over to the long table, talking about what they could build to solve the challenge.

Amelia Bedelia stood next to her friend Penny. "Have you seen the cat?" she whispered.

"What cat?" asked Penny.

All around them, kids were brainstorming and examining the objects on the table. Skip was using duct tape to attach several cardboard tubes together. Joy had picked up a long piece of wood and was stacking up blocks to make a ramp. Heather was wrapping string

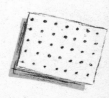

around a rubber ball. Everybody seemed to be concentrating on their projects.

But Amelia Bedelia really couldn't concentrate when there was a cat that might need her help.

She glanced around the room again. She bent down to peer under all the desks. No cat.

"Are you looking for dust bunnies?" Penny asked her.

Amelia Bedelia straightened up and shook her head. "No!" she whispered. "The cat!"

There was only one place left to look. If there was a cat in the science room, it must be behind Ms. Garcia's desk.

While Ms. Garcia was talking to Holly and Clay, Amelia Bedelia took a chance.

She darted across the room and slipped down behind Ms. Garcia's desk. Crouching, she pushed Ms. Garcia's chair aside and peered into the space beneath the desk.

No cat.

What about the big desk drawers? Could a cat could be hiding in there? Amelia Bedelia tugged one open and peeked in. It was full of school supplies. No cat.

"Amelia Bedelia?" said a voice behind her. "What are you doing?"

Chapter 2

Moving Your Marbles
(without losing your marbles)

Amelia Bedelia jumped, smacking the top of her head on the desk. *EEEE-OW! EEEE-OW! EEEE-OW!* The desk drawer slipped out of her hand and thumped shut.

Was she in trouble?

Nope, mainly because the person standing over her wasn't Ms. Garcia. It was Penny, gazing at Amelia Bedelia

13

wide-eyed through her glasses.

"Amelia Bedelia," whispered Penny. "Come on! Everybody got a head start on us. We only have a few more minutes to make something!"

She grabbed Amelia Bedelia's arm and pulled her back over to the maker table. Ms. Garcia was watching Clay demonstrate a slingshot he'd made with some sticks and rubber bands.

Everybody else was already testing their inventions and even making improvements. Amelia Bedelia and Penny had some catching up to do.

Amelia Bedelia needed a good idea.

There was a big cardboard box in the middle of the table. She started with that. She put the box on the floor and jumped into it. She counted to ten, then she hopped out.

No new ideas popped into her brain. She frowned. Weird. Why wasn't this working? She stepped back into the box.

"Amelia Bedelia, what are you doing?" said a voice behind her. This time it *was* Ms. Garcia.

Amelia Bedelia stepped back out of the box. "I'm thinking outside the box," she said.

Ms. Garcia smiled. "Amelia Bedelia, you're very good at

coming up with great ideas. You are a great thinker. You don't need a box. All you need is your brain! Now ready, set, think!"

Ms. Garcia moved around the table to check on Joy's progress. Joy had used a thin piece of wood to build a ramp. She was trying to roll a marble down it. But her ramp was too steep, and the marble kept veering off to one side or the other.

"Failure is a part of invention," Ms. Garcia said. "Remember, a good inventor is always ready to go back to the drawing board!"

Amelia Bedelia smiled. Exactly! She reached across the table and grabbed a

board just like the one Joy was using. She found a pencil. Then she went to work.

The science room was quiet except for the sound of marbles rolling, tape unrolling, and Harriet scampering on her wheel. Amelia Bedelia concentrated on her board, sketching out her idea.

"Anyone have an invention ready to go?" Ms. Garcia finally asked, breaking the silence.

Amelia Bedelia raised her hand.

"Okay, come over here and show us all!" said Ms. Garcia, pointing to a small table on the other side of the science room. Five white marbles sat on the table. Ms. Garcia had used masking tape to mark off a distance of twelve inches.

"Can you get the marbles from here to there without touching them?" Ms. Garcia pointed to the start line and the finish line.

Amelia Bedelia nodded as her classmates gathered all around.

She kneeled and slipped her board underneath two of the table legs.

Now the table was tilted, with one end, the end closest to the starting line, a little bit higher than the other. Slowly the marbles began to roll across the surface of the table. When they had almost reached the twelve-inch mark, Amelia Bedelia slipped her board out from under the table legs, and the marbles rolled to a stop.

"Whoa! You did it!" said Clay, giving Amelia Bedelia a high five.

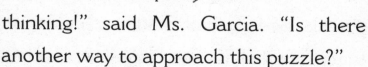

"I went back to the drawing board!" she said. "And it worked!"

Skip had made a suction tube with paper-towel rolls and a turkey baster. But he could only get one marble to the finish line. "Keep thinking!" said Ms. Garcia. "Is there another way to approach this puzzle?"

Joy had constructed a ramp out of a board and blocks, and she had taped together a paper scoop to pick up the marbles so she could place them on the top of the ramp. But three of her marbles fell off the ramp before they'd moved twelve inches. "Keep making improvements," said Ms. Garcia. "How can you slow the momentum of a marble?"

Cliff's slingshot was very good at moving the marbles, but he had to pick them up to put them in it. "How can you solve that?" said Ms. Garcia. "Turn the problem over in your mind."

Out of all the kids in the class, only Amelia Bedelia had made an invention that moved all five marbles twelve inches without her touching them once.

When the bell finally rang for recess, everyone ran outside. Joy grabbed a ball, and Amelia Bedelia, Dawn, Skip, Wade, Joy, and Penny raced to the foursquare court. It was their favorite recess game.

SMACK! Amelia Bedelia whacked the ball as hard as she could. It bounded into Skip's square, and he whacked it back to her. *SMACK!*

SMACK! SMACK! SMACK!

SMACK!

SMACK! *SMACK!* *SMACK!*

The ball bounced from Skip to Penny to Joy to Amelia Bedelia. Back to Joy . . . back to Amelia Bedelia . . . who gave it the hardest whack she could.

SMACK! SMACK! SMACK!

SMACK! SMACK. SMACK!

The ball whizzed into Penny's square, bounced once, and kept going. Penny lunged for it, but missed. She was out!

The ball was out, too—out of the foursquare court. It rolled over the playground and bounded down a little hill, scattering wood chips.

"I'll get it!" yelled Amelia Bedelia, chasing after the ball.

The ball gained speed as it headed down the hill, just as the marbles had gotten faster when they'd headed down Joy's ramp. It bounced across a little patch of grass and rolled between some trees in the far corner of the playground.

Amelia Bedelia plunged right after it.

Chapter 3

"Curiosity killed the Cat . . ."

It was so shady under the trees, and it felt nice and cool. Amelia Bedelia spotted the ball under a bush. She grabbed it and turned to run back to the game.

"Oooooow!"

A high-pitched cry echoed through the trees.

"Ooooooowwwwww!" *Ooooooowwww*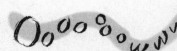

The cry sent a shiver through Amelia Bedelia.

She did not believe in ghosts. But if ghosts were real and if ghosts were haunting the playground at Oak Tree Elementary, she was pretty sure they would sound like that.

"Amelia Bedelia? Are you okay?" said a voice behind her.

Amelia Bedelia jumped. She whipped around to see Penny, who had followed her.

"What's taking so long?" asked Penny.

"I heard a spooky noise," said Amelia Bedelia.

Penny's eyes got wide. "What noise?" she asked.

"*Oooooowwwww . . .*"

$O_oo^{OO}_{o^O}_{o_w}^{w^{w^{w^w}}}$

"That noise," said
Amelia Bedelia. It sounded
as if it was coming from
somewhere high up in
the air.

"Oooooowwwww . . ."

Penny and Amelia Bedelia looked
at each other. "What *is* that?" Penny
whispered.

Now Amelia Bedelia was getting really
nervous. But she was curious, too. "Let's
find out!" she whispered back.

"I don't know." Penny shook her head.
"My mom always says curiosity
killed the cat."

"We're not cats!" said
Amelia Bedelia. "Come on!"

Amelia Bedelia tiptoed around a tree trunk, right toward the place where the sound had come from. Penny followed her, and Amelia Bedelia was glad about that. If you are investigating a spooky noise, it's good to have a friend with you.

They picked their way over fallen branches and clumps of grass. When they got very close to the fence that separated the playground from the street —"Oooooowwwww!"—they heard the sound again, right above their heads. Penny gasped. Amelia Bedelia gulped.

They both looked up. Then they looked at each other. They both grinned.

27

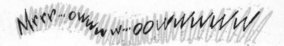

"A cat!" said Amelia Bedelia.

Sure enough, there was a cat up in the tree. The cat was white with orange and black spots. It didn't look like a very big cat. More like a half-grown kitten. It clung to the bark of the maple tree with all four paws.

"Meeeeee-ooooooooow!" it yowled.

"I think it's stuck," said Amelia Bedelia. "Here, kitty kitty, come on down!"

"I don't think it knows how," said Penny. "Cats are good at climbing up, but not so good at coming back down. I don't think it can get out of the tree."

"It's practically a baby," said Amelia Bedelia. "It looks scared."

"We have to help it," said Penny. "It's so cute!"

Amelia Bedelia nodded. "That cat has a problem, and we need to invent a solution," she said.

"Hey, Penny! Hey, Amelia Bedelia! What's going on?" Skip had come into the trees after them. "Did you find the ball?" he asked.

"Yup," said Amelia Bedelia, pointing at the leafy top of the maple tree. "And look what else we found!"

"Aw, poor girl," said Skip, looking up.

calico cat

"How do you know it's a girl?" asked Penny.

"Because it's a calico," said Skip. "It's orange and black and white. Almost all calicos are girls. How are we going to get it down?"

"We need to invent something!" said Amelia Bedelia.

A few minutes later Joy, Angel, Dawn, and Wade arrived, crowding around the base of the tree and looking up at the kitten. Everyone was doing their best to brainstorm ideas to rescue the cat.

"We need something long to poke it with!" said Wade. "Then it will jump down and we can catch it." He and Joy went searching for a long stick. But the longest one they could find didn't even reach halfway up the tree trunk.

"It's too short," said Penny. "Anyway, if we poke her, it might hurt and make her scramble up higher."

"If we take off our jackets and hoodies, we could make a pile at the bottom of the tree," said Joy. "Then she'll have a soft place to land."

Everybody agreed that was a good idea, and soon jackets and sweatshirts were piled at the base of the tree.

"Mrrr—owwww—oowwwww!" The cat didn't move.

"My mom built me a tree house in the backyard," said Dawn. "She nailed pieces of board to the trunk, like steps, so that I could climb up. If we had a hammer, we could do that."

But they didn't have a hammer or nails.

"We need a big trampoline!" said Joy.

"Then we could jump high enough to grab her!"

But they didn't have a trampoline, either.

"I have an idea!" said Penny. She began talking like a cat. "Meow! Meow! Meow! Meow!"

"Why are you meowing?" asked Amelia Bedelia.

"If she thinks her friends are down here waiting to play with her," said Penny, "maybe she'll come down." MEOW!

"Good idea!" said Dawn. MEOW!

"MEOW! MEOW!"

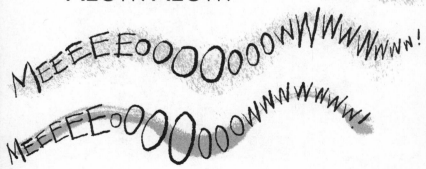

MEEEEOOOOOOOWWWWWww!

MEEEEOOOOOOOOWWWWWW!

MEOW! MEOW! MEOW! MEOW

Everyone meowed as loudly as they could.

MEC

MEOW! The cat turned her head and stared at them. She blinked. She meowed even more loudly herself. But she didn't climb down. Instead, she sat back and started to lick her paw.

MEOW! MEOW! MEOW! MEOW! MEO

EOW! MEO

Meoww Meow! Meow Meow Meoww Meeoww

That gave Amelia Bedelia another idea.

The cat wouldn't come down because of what she heard—but maybe she'd come down because of what she smelled.

"Wait!" said Amelia Bedelia. "I'll be right back!"

Amelia Bedelia raced across the playground. She darted into the building. They weren't supposed to go inside at recess, but she'd have to break that rule, or at least bend it a little.

There was something in Amelia Bedelia's locker that might just save the day.

Chapter 4

Thinking Outside the Can

When Amelia Bedelia told Mr. Jack, the Oak Tree Elementary custodian, that she had to go inside for an emergency, he nodded and let her in.

"Be quick about it," he said. "Recess is almost over."

He did not ask her what the emergency was. That was good because Amelia Bedelia didn't have time to explain.

She raced to her locker, pulled her lunch box out of her backpack, then ran back outside.

"Thanks, Mr. Jack!" she yelled as she sprinted across the playground. She skidded to a stop under the tree.

"Lunch?" asked Joy. "Amelia Bedelia, it isn't lunchtime."

"I know that," panted Amelia Bedelia. "But maybe the cat doesn't."

She opened up her lunch box and unwrapped her sandwich. She peeled off the top piece of bread. A certain smell drifted into the air. It was a smell that

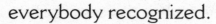

everybody recognized.

"Tuna fish!" exclaimed Joy. "Amelia Bedelia, what a great idea!"

"Definitely thinking outside the box," agreed Skip. "The lunch box, that is."

"And outside the tuna fish can," said Amelia Bedelia. She waved the open face of her sandwich in the air, then put it down next to the pile of sweatshirts and jackets. Everybody backed away, watching quietly.

Tuna

"Cross your fingers," whispered Penny.

The cat turned her head. Her nose and whiskers twitched. She seemed very interested in the aroma of tuna fish floating through the air.

S-L-O-W-L-Y, almost in slow motion, the cat lifted one paw and put it down a little lower on the trunk. Bit by bit, she began to ease her way back down the tree.

"Amelia Bedelia, you're a genius!" whispered Penny.

"She's an inventor!" whispered Joy.

Just then, the cat suddenly slipped, slithering several inches down the trunk with a tiny, frightened *mew*. Amelia *Mew*

Meee-ooow!

Bedelia and her friends gasped. They all held their breath. If she fell, would she land on the soft jackets and sweatshirts? Would she survive such a drop?

The cat didn't land on the pile of clothing. She landed on a lower branch and crouched there. "Meee-*ooow!*" She put her nose in the air to smell the tuna fish again, but she didn't move.

And didn't move.

And didn't move.

"I think she's more scared than ever," Penny said. "It was a really good idea, Amelia Bedelia, but I don't think it's going to work. Maybe we—"

"What is going on here? The bell rang three minutes ago!"

Everybody jumped and turned to see Mr. Jack frowning at them.

"What's the matter—cat got your tongues?" he asked.

Amelia Bedelia looked around at her friends. "Our cat doesn't have anybody's tongue," she said. "Except her own, I guess."

"Cat? What cat?" asked Mr. Jack.

"That cat," said Amelia Bedelia, pointing up at the kitten.

Mr. Jack looked up. "Well, would you look at that!" he said. He smiled. "Poor kitty."

"We've been trying
to get her out of the tree,"
said Amelia Bedelia.

"But we can't find a stick long
enough and we don't have a hammer or
nails or a trampoline and she won't even
come down for tuna fish!" said Penny.

Mr. Jack laughed. "Well, I don't have a
trampoline, either. I do have a hammer and
nails, but I think there's a simpler solution
to this problem. I'll be right back."

Chapter 5

Out on a Limb

Mr. Jack returned a few minutes later with a long ladder balanced on his shoulder and their teacher, Mrs. Shauk, following behind him. Mr. Jack leaned the ladder against the tree trunk. He put both hands and one foot on the ladder and then hesitated.

"I hate to admit it," he said. "But when it comes to heights, I'm a real scaredy-cat."

Amelia Bedelia looked at Mr. Jack and frowned. He didn't have pointy ears, long whiskers, or a tail. She didn't see how he could be a scaredy-cat or a brave cat or any kind of cat at all.

"I'm pretty skittish about heights myself," said Mrs. Shauk.

"I'll do it!" said Amelia Bedelia. She didn't mind heights. She liked climbing trees. And she loved animals.

"Okay, up you go," Mrs. Shauk said. "Climb up and get the cat if you can. Just go slowly and hold on tight!"

Amelia Bedelia tucked the tuna-fish sandwich into her pocket and headed up the ladder.

The first few steps were no problem. But then she began to see what Mr. Jack was talking about. She glanced down. The ground was pretty far away and getting farther with each rung. Even though Mr. Jack was holding the ladder steady, it still sagged and bounced a bit under her weight.

Was she a scaredy-cat? Maybe so. She almost felt as if a tail were about to sprout from *her* spine, as if her ears were getting points and growing soft fur.

"You can do it, Amelia Bedelia!" shouted Joy.

"Keep going!" yelled Penny. "Our cat is counting on you!"

Amelia Bedelia held on tightly and kept climbing. At last she reached the branch where the cat was crouched.

Amelia Bedelia offered a tiny taste of tuna fish to the cat. The cat took a bite

and licked her lips, looking at Amelia
Bedelia as if to say, "Thank you." Moving
carefully and slowly, Amelia Bedelia
reached out to pick her up. "Here, kitty
kitty," she whispered.

The cat did not want to be picked
up. It scooted along the branch, getting
farther away from the trunk of the tree

and farther away from Amelia Bedelia.

"Don't go out on a limb, kitty!" Amelia Bedelia pleaded. She held out a bigger piece of tuna fish.

But the cat was no longer interested. She scampered back to the trunk and clawed her way up to a branch just above Amelia Bedelia's head.

Everybody on the ground below let out a groan. So did Amelia Bedelia. But there was nothing for Amelia Bedelia to do but climb back down the ladder.

"What can we do now?" she asked when she was on solid ground again.

"Back to the drawing board, I think," said Mrs. Shauk.

"I'll go get mine," said Amelia Bedelia.

"No, thank you," said Mrs. Shauk, holding the back of Amelia Bedelia's hoodie to slow her down. "When at first you don't succeed, define the problem."

"The problem is that our ladder isn't long enough," said Joy.

"Exactly right," said Mrs. Shauk.

"It's the longest one I have," said Mr. Jack.

"Some people in this town have ladders that are much longer," said Mrs. Shauk.

The kids looked at one another and shrugged.

Mr. Jack made the sound of a siren.

"A fire truck!" said Penny.

"Right. I think it's time to call the fire department," said Mrs. Shauk.

"I'll go pull the fire alarm!" said Wade.

"No, I can!" said Joy.

"I'll do it!" said Amelia Bedelia.

"I think a phone call will do," said Mrs. Shauk. "I don't want anyone to get hurt. This situation is not an emergency."

"It is for the cat!" said Penny.

"It's a catastrophe!" said Amelia Bedelia.

Chapter 6

One Fire Truck, Hold the Siren

Amelia Bedelia had seen the town fire truck in a parade before, but she had never seen it at her school. The firefighters did not turn on the siren because it wasn't an emergency, but it was still exciting to

see the bright red fire truck pull up to Oak Tree Elementary. While Mrs. Shauk and Mr. Jack explained the problem and kids in other classrooms watched out their windows, Amelia Bedelia and her friends raced back across the playground. They waited for the fire truck as it circled around to the street nearest the maple tree.

Finally the truck pulled up beside the fence that separated the playground from the street. One of the firefighters came over to the fence. "Please keep the kids

at a safe distance for now," she told Mrs. Shauk. "And later on, we'll let them take a look in the truck if they want to."

"We want to!" yelled Clay. He darted toward the fire truck and began climbing the fence. Mrs. Shauk pulled him back. "It's like herding cats!" she said.

"I can see that!" said the other firefighter, who was driving the truck.

Maybe Mrs. Shauk needs a lasso, thought Amelia Bedelia. *And a cowboy hat.* She started to giggle. The legendary Hawk, herding cats on the prairie!

"Thank you, Lieutenant Johnson,"

said Mrs. Shauk. "I'm sure my class would love to see the fire truck—*if* they can listen to directions now."

Amelia Bedelia reached over the fence and offered Lieutenant Johnson what was left of her tuna-fish sandwich.

"No, thank you," the firefighter said. "I already ate lunch."

"It's for the cat," said Amelia Bedelia. "To lure her down. She likes tuna fish."

"Ah-ha! Got it!" Lieutenant Johnson grinned and took the sandwich. "Great

54

MEOW.   MEOW!   MEOW!

thinking—you're the cat's meow!"

"Oh, I tried that," said Amelia Bedelia. "It didn't work, but I can try again."

Amelia Bedelia walked over to the maple tree. "Meow," she called softly, looking up at the cat. "Meow, meow?"

"Amelia Bedelia," said Penny. "What are you doing?"

MEOW!

MEOW!

"Lieutenant Johnson told me to," said Amelia Bedelia.

"Really?" said Penny. "But we tried that." Penny shrugged. "Okay. I'll help!"

"Meow, meeee-ooowwwww! *MEEE-OOOOWWWWW!*" meeeeeee-OOOOoooooow

Amelia Bedelia and Penny meowed together. Soon Joy, Dawn, and Skip joined in.

MEOW! MEOW! MEOW! MEOW!

MEOW! MEOW! MEOW! MEOW

MEOW!   MEOW!   MEOW

"Hey, kids, what are you doing?" asked Mrs. Shauk.

"We're the cat's meows!" said Amelia Bedelia. "Meeee-OW!"

From high in the tree, the cat replied. "Meeeeowwwww!"

"Look, the ladder's   Meee-ooow! going up!" yelled Cliff.

The big ladder on the back of the truck began to unfold and stretch toward the tree. It inched closer and closer to the branch where the cat was sitting. Once it was locked into position, Lieutenant Johnson began to climb. She reached the cat's branch, and Amelia Bedelia held her breath.

Lieutenant Johnson pulled Amelia

Bedelia's sandwich out of her pocket and offered it to the cat. The cat inched toward her. She put her nose in the air and sniffed. Then she began to nibble the tuna fish.

The firefighter let the cat eat for a few seconds. Then she quickly scooped her up, tucked her under one arm, and headed back down the ladder.

When they reached the ground, the class clapped and cheered.

"What an excellent rescue operation!" said Mrs. Shauk. "Thank you, Lieutenant, very much."

"You're welcome!" said

Lieutenant Johnson. "Now, who wants to see the fire truck?"

The cat seemed really happy to be out of the tree. At least as happy as a cat can be. While Amelia Bedelia's friends toured the truck, Amelia Bedelia cuddled the cat and fed her bits of tuna. The cat purred so loudly that her whole body trembled. Amelia Bedelia wondered where the cat lived.

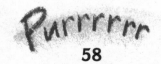

Did she belong to a family? Was someone searching for her right now?

Everybody got a chance to look in the back of the fire truck, to see the uniforms and hats and hoses and pump controls, and even to sit in the driver's seat up front. Then they thanked the firefighters and watched as the truck pulled away.

"That was so cool!" said Clay. He gave Cliff a high five.

"I think that's enough problem-solving for one day," said Mrs. Shauk. "It's time to head back."

Everyone groaned. Even Mr. Jack.

"But, young lady," said Mrs. Shauk to

Amelia Bedelia, "you can't bring that cat with you!"

Amelia Bedelia looked down at the purring cat. The cat's eyes were tightly closed, and she sounded like a tiny motor.

"But I can't just let her go!" Amelia Bedelia said.

"Does she have a tag on her collar?" asked Mrs. Shauk.

"She doesn't even have a  collar," said Amelia Bedelia.

"She's probably a stray, then," said Mrs. Shauk. "We'll have to call the animal shelter."

Amelia Bedelia did not like that idea one bit. She'd been to the animal shelter

once before, when she adopted her dog, Finally. She knew that the people there really cared about animals, but still, it was not like living in a home with a family.

"The cat really likes you, Amelia Bedelia," Penny said. "You should take her home with you."

"Thanks, Penny!" said Amelia Bedelia. "That's the perfect solution!"

Chapter 7

Pleased to Meet You . . . Ahh-choo!

After the last bell rang, Amelia Bedelia rushed to get the cat from Mr. Jack, who was cat sitting her. Then Amelia Bedelia cuddled the cat against her sweatshirt and carried her home.

When she opened the front door, her dog, Finally, bounded to greet her, just like always. But this time Finally skidded to a

stop and stared in astonishment at the cat in Amelia Bedelia's arms.

"WOOF-WOOF-Grrrr."

"Finally, this is our new cat," said Amelia Bedelia. "Be nice!"

She put the cat down on the floor. Finally barked again. It was as if she was saying, "What is *that*? And why did you bring it to *my* house?"

The cat didn't seem one bit scared. She shook herself a little. Her tail was very high and quivering. She took a few steps forward and sniffed at Finally's nose. Then she started to purr. Finally put her nose down and sniffed the cat's head and all along her back.

purrrr

The cat arched her back. She put her head up and rubbed it against Finally's face.

Finally's tail started to wag—slow at first, then faster.

Purr, wag. *Purr-rrrr*, wag, wag, wag.

Amelia Bedelia smiled. Her two pets were going to be friends!

Just then Amelia Bedelia's mother came into the front hall. "Amelia Bedelia, what's *that*?" she asked, pointing to the cat.

Then she sneezed so loudy that Amelia Bedelia, Finally, and the cat all jumped.

Kids do not always know everything about their parents. Amelia Bedelia did not know that her mother had been the school spelling bee champion when she was in third grade or that her mother had once dyed her hair bright blue in college. And she did not know that her mother was allergic to cats.

Amelia Bedelia apologized for bringing home a cat without asking. Her father drove to the drugstore to get some allergy medicine. And her mother said that Amelia Bedelia could keep the cat for five days.

"But no longer than five days," said

her mother. "AHH—Choo!"

Five days was not a very long time to find a perfect home for the cat. Amelia Bedelia knew that she was going to need some help.

The next morning, Amelia Bedelia hurried to Mrs. Shauk's classroom as soon as the bell rang. They always began their class with announcements and sharing, and Amelia Bedelia's hand shot up right away. She squirmed in her seat and wiggled her fingers, hoping to catch the Hawk's eye.

"Amelia Bedelia, you're acting

like a cat on a hot tin roof!" said Mrs. Shauk. "Did you have something to share with the class?"

Amelia Bedelia nodded. She told everyone about her mother. "I need to find a new home for the cat," she explained. "Who else can take her?"

"I will!" said Penny.

"Yes!" said Angel.

"Sure thing!" said Skip.

Amelia Bedelia beamed. Her friends were the best! She hadn't thought that finding a solution to her problem would be this easy.

"Very well, class," said Mrs. Shauk. "If you are

interested in taking the cat, have your parents contact Amelia Bedelia's parents. And now, it's time for your vocabulary quiz."

All that evening, Amelia Bedelia waited for Angel or Penny or Skip to call. But the phone didn't ring once. Not once.

That night, Amelia Bedelia slept with Finally at the foot of her bed and the cat curled up beside her, purring loudly in her ear.

Purrrrrr

At school the next morning, no one looked very cheerful. Amelia Bedelia and her friends met outside at the student lounge—which was really the stump of a very special tree—at recess.

"My mom said our building has a rule that only pets in cages are allowed," said Angel. She shrugged sadly. "My python is

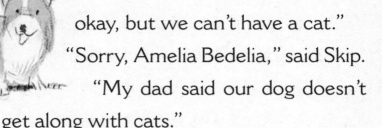

okay, but we can't have a cat."

"Sorry, Amelia Bedelia," said Skip.
"My dad said our dog doesn't get along with cats."

"My parents said that we already have two cats. Plus three gerbils and an aquarium full of fish," said Penny. "They said no more pets until I graduate from college and have my own apartment."

"We can't wait that long," said Amelia Bedelia.

It turned out that none of the kids in Mrs. Shauk's class were able to give the cat a home. Either someone was allergic to cats or they already had cats or dogs or

guinea pigs or rabbits. Some lived in places that did not allow pets.

No one could take the cat. And now they only had four days to find the perfect home.

"There's got to be somebody who wants such a sweet cat!" said Penny. "We just have to find the right person."

"We can advertise!" said Amelia Bedelia. "That's what my dad always says to do."

"But we're just kids," said Joy. "How are we going to advertise? It's not like we can make a commercial and get it on TV."

"We can make posters," said Amelia Bedelia. "We can put them up all over town!"

Mr. Forest, the art teacher, was happy for Amelia Bedelia and her friends to make posters during their art period. They drew pictures of the cat and brainstormed slogans that would catch people's eye, making them want to give the cat a home.

Amelia Bedelia drew a picture of a calico cat curled up in a ball with her paw over her nose. PURRRRRRRFECT PET! she wrote

above her curled-up cat.

"Hey!" said Cliff. "You're a copycat, Amelia Bedelia."

Amelia Bedelia had not even looked at Cliff's poster. Now when she did, she

saw that he had drawn a cat curled up in a ball, just like hers. But that didn't mean that she'd copied him. If he'd drawn a poodle and she'd drawn a Great Dane, he'd probably call her a copy dog.

"I didn't copy you," she said. "I just drew the cat."

"That can happen," said Mr. Forest, smiling. "Sometimes artists have similar ideas, but their art will still look different when they are done. See, Cliff, your cat

CAT by PICASSO

CAT by ANDY WARHOL

73

75

has its eyes open, and Amelia Bedelia drew hers with its eyes shut. No two artists will ever draw the same thing in *exactly* the same way. Every work of art is unique. Nobody can be a copycat, Cliff, even if they try to be."

After school, Amelia Bedelia got permission from her mother to go out with Joy and Penny to put the posters up around the neighborhood. "Don't stay out too long," her mother told them with a sneeze. "It's getting very cloudy. It looks like rain."

The girls were rushing to put up as many posters as possible. They went to Pete's Diner first, and after checking with Pete to make sure it was okay, they got to work taping a poster to the front door. Amelia Bedelia was sticking the last piece of tape to the glass when a woman hurrying into the diner nearly bumped into her.

"Oops! Excuse me!" the woman said.

"No problem," said Amelia Bedelia. The woman looked familiar, but Amelia Bedelia wasn't sure where she might have seen her before.

The woman looked at the poster and smiled. "That's the cat that was in the tree near the elementary school, isn't it?" she asked.

"It is!" said Amelia Bedelia. How could this woman know that? Looking at her more closely, it dawned on Amelia Bedelia.

"Hi, Lieutenant Johnson!" she said.

"Wow!" said Joy. "We didn't recognize you without your uniform."

Lieutenant Johnson laughed. "That happens a lot," she said. "I'm glad you're

trying to find a home for that sweet cat. Good luck!"

"Thanks!" said the girls, and they hurried on their way. They went to the library and put a poster on the bulletin board. They put a poster up on the community board outside the grocery store, too. And at the park. They posted some posters around the school, attaching several to the fence with tape.

Then they were out of posters. Out of tape. And totally out of time.

From far away came a low grumble of thunder. A cold drop of rain splashed down on Amelia Bedelia's nose.

"Let's go home!" said Joy. "I hope the posters work!"

"I hope your phone rings soon," said Penny. "Cross your fingers!"

Amelia Bedelia crossed her fingers and waved goodbye to her friends before racing home herself.

Chapter 8

The Cat Turns into a Pumpkin

By the time Amelia Bedelia got home, her hair was dripping, her shirt was soggy, and her shoes were squelching.

"Look what the cat dragged in!" said her father when she opened the front door.

"What?" Amelia Bedelia looked around. Did the cat get out? Did

she bring something back inside to play with?"

"I meant you!" said her father.

"But the cat didn't drag me in," said Amelia Bedelia. "I walked home. I mean, I ran home."

"I can see that—and you got soaking wet," said her father. "Go change into dry clothes."

Amelia Bedelia ran upstairs. She found Finally and the cat curled up together on her bed. Finally was snoring and the cat

was purring. They were nearly as loud as the storm outside.

"Hello, Finally! Hello, cat!" she said.

Amelia Bedelia dried her hair, put on dry clothes, and tossed her wet things in the hamper. She settled onto the bed and waited for the phone to ring. Surely someone would see one of their posters soon and call her. Surely someone would want to adopt such a sweet and friendly cat.

As she waited, Amelia Bedelia scratched Finally with one hand and the cat with the other. She wished she could keep the cat. She was so cute and soft! It wasn't nice to keep thinking of the cat as simply the cat, though. She needed a name.

Her orange-and-black fur made Amelia Bedelia think about Halloween. And the way the cat was curled up with just the tip of her tail sticking out reminded Amelia Bedelia of a pumpkin with a stem.

That's it! Pumpkin! It was the perfect name!

"Hello, Finally! Hello, Pumpkin!" she said.

Now all Pumpkin needed was a perfect home. But it seemed as if a home was going to be harder to find than a name, because the phone did not ring all afternoon.

It did not ring during dinner.

It did not ring when Amelia Bedelia was doing her homework.

It did not ring before bedtime.

Two days out of five were gone, and Pumpkin still did not have a home.

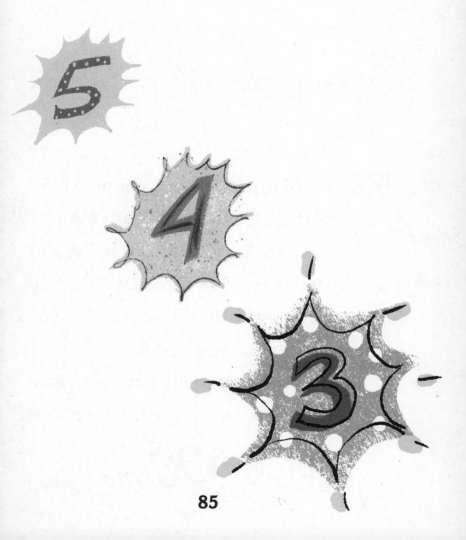

Chapter 9

Coupons for a Cat

chirp

chirp

chirp

Meow! Meow! Chirp, chirp, chirp! Meow! MEEEEOOOOOWWWW!

Amelia Bedelia woke up. Pumpkin was sitting on the windowsill watching a bird in the tree outside her window. The sun was shining, drying up puddles.

When Amelia Bedelia got to school, she began to understand why the phone

MEEEEEE-OOOOOOOOW!

hadn't rung. The posters that she and Penny and Joy had taped up around the playground had been ruined by the rain. The paint and ink had run, and the paper was soggy and torn. Nobody could see how cute Pumpkin was—and nobody could read the phone number.

"Oh, no," said Penny when she jumped off the bus. "After all our hard work!"

Penny and Amelia Bedelia stared at the posters—or what was left of them.

"It just means we have to work harder and find a new solution," said Amelia Bedelia. "We need to put an ad someplace where it can't be washed away."

"But where?" asked Penny.

"I know," said Amelia Bedelia. "In the newspaper!"

At recess, Amelia Bedelia's friends gathered around the stump table while Amelia Bedelia, Penny, and Joy explained what had happened to the posters.

"My dad always says the more people who see your ad, the better," said Amelia Bedelia. "If we put an ad in the newspaper, everyone who lives in this town will see it. Somebody will want to take Pumpkin home."

"Cool, but who is Pumpkin?" asked Clay.

"The cat," said Amelia Bedelia.

"Amelia Bedelia named the cat Pumpkin," said Penny.

"That's the perfect name!" said Joy.

"But doesn't it cost a lot to put an ad in the paper?" asked Angel.

"Not really," said Amelia Bedelia. "Mr. B helped me look it up on the library computer. We can buy a small  ad for two hundred dollars."

Amelia Bedelia's friends stared back at her blankly.

"Amelia Bedelia, we don't have two hundred dollars," said Skip.

"We can earn it," said Amelia Bedelia.

"How?" asked Penny. "My allowance is only five dollars a week."

"So is mine," said Amelia Bedelia. "But there are twenty kids in our class. So that's one hundred dollars. What if we each ask our parents to give us double the chores?"

Her friends started nodding. That seemed possible.

"We can even ask

90

our neighbors or grandparents if they need chores done," said Cliff.

"I know, we can make chore coupon books!" said Joy.

"That's a great idea!" said Penny.

After lunch, Joy got two pieces of

fold ←   fold ↩   unfold & cut

×2 =

Decide on your chores and decorate your coupons!

WASH DISHES

MOW LAWN

Staple together

paper and folded them in half, then in half again. That made eight small rectangles.

On each rectangle she wrote a chore. Skip, who was very good at drawing, made a sketch of each chore and created a cover for the coupon book.

"See, if we each sell one chore coupon book, we'll have the money we need for the ad," Joy explained.

"It's a really good invention," said Amelia Bedelia. "And it's going to work—I know it will."

Mrs. Roman said they could use the office copier to make twenty chore books, plus some extras. At the end of the day, they handed them out. Every kid in Mrs. Shauk's class agreed to try to convince someone to buy one. They would bring the money to Amelia Bedelia tomorrow.

***

At dinner that night, Amelia Bedelia showed her parents her chore coupon books and told them about the plans to raise money for an ad.

"You always say free advertising is the best kind," she told her father. "But two-hundred-dollar advertising is still pretty good, right? Plus it will be dry."

"It definitely is," agreed her father. "Much better than five-hundred-dollar advertising . . . or two-thousand-dollar advertising . . . or—"

"We get the idea, honey," said Amelia Bedelia's mother, blowing her nose. "The best thing about this coupon book is that it guarantees no complaining. I'll take two!"

"So far, so good," said Amelia Bedelia's father to Amelia Bedelia.

Amelia Bedelia's mother took two ten-dollar bills from her purse and gave them to Amelia Bedelia.

"Thanks, Mom!" said Amelia Bedelia. She got up from the table and tucked the money into her backpack. "I'm going to go play with Pumpkin."

"Oh, cool your jets," said her mother, ripping a page out of the coupon book and handing it to Amelia Bedelia with a smile.

"I don't have any," said Amelia Bedelia looking at the coupon. Wash dishes, it said.

"Better get to work," her father said. "We want to see if you're worth your salt!"

"No thanks, Daddy. Mom already gave me money," said Amelia Bedelia. "Do I have to wash the dishes right now? I was going to play with Pumpkin and Finally."

"No whining or complaining," said her mother. "That's the guarantee, right?"

"Right," agreed Amelia Bedelia.

While Amelia Bedelia's parents settled down in the living room to watch TV, Amelia Bedelia cleared the table and stacked the dirty dishes next to the sink. Suddenly she was not so sure it was such a good thing that her parents had bought two coupon books. Maybe one would have been enough.

But it was worth it if it helped to find Pumpkin a good home!

Chapter 10

Extra! Extra! Read All About ~~It~~ Pumpkin

The coupon books were a big hit. Some parents, like Amelia Bedelia's, had purchased more than one. When Amelia Bedelia counted the money, there was enough for the ad, and a little left over.

Amelia Bedelia and Skip had worked all recess on the ad. Skip had drawn a picture of Pumpkin, looking very friendly

and a little lonely, and Amelia Bedelia had written the words:

SWEET CAT NEEDS GOOD HOME!! EXCELLENT AT PURRING, VERY CUTE AND LOVES TO CUDDLE. PLEASE CALL 555-5555. EMERGENCY! NO TIME TO WASTE!

After school, Amelia Bedelia, Skip, Penny, and Joy hurried downtown, past Pete's Diner and the library, to a bright green door. On it was written DAILY GAZETTE—WHAT'S HAPPENING AROUND TOWN.

They pushed the door open and went inside.

tap-tap-tap-tap-tap

Tap-tap-tap-tap-tap! *tap-tap-tap-tap-ta*

Amelia Bedelia looked around. She had never been inside a newspaper office before. The desks had computers on them and papers piled here and there. A woman who was typing looked up and smiled.

"May I help you?" she asked.

"We want to—" said Skip.

"We need a—" said Penny.

"Do you have a—" said Joy.

They all stopped at once, uncertain.

"Come on, let the cat out of the bag," said the woman, smiling.

"We didn't bring the cat," said Amelia Bedelia.

"What cat?" the woman asked.

"Pumpkin," said Amelia Bedelia.

"The one the ad is for," said Joy.

The woman shook her head. "What ad?" she asked.

"The one we want to put in the paper," said Amelia Bedelia. She showed the woman their ad.

"So you're trying to find a new home

for your cat?" the woman asked, studying the ad.

"She's not really my cat," said Amelia Bedelia. She explained how they'd found the cat on the playground. Penny told how they'd tried to get the cat out of the tree. Joy explained that the fire truck had to come. Skip described how Lieutenant Johnson had lured the cat down with

Amelia Bedelia's tuna-fish sandwich.

The woman listened. Her eyes got rounder and rounder.

"I think you've made a mistake," she said. "You don't want to place an ad."

"Yes, we do," said Amelia Bedelia. "We have two hundred and forty dollars, so we can afford it."

The woman smiled. "I'm sure you can, but you don't need an ad. This is news! I want to write a story for the paper about Pumpkin the cat and how the students at Oak Tree Elementary rescued her. You kids are the cat's pajamas!"

Amelia Bedelia looked at her clothes. She had pajamas with cats on them at

home, but she wasn't wearing them. She had on leggings and a stripy skirt and a shirt with flowers on it and a purple jacket with a hood.

"These aren't my pajamas," she said. "And mine are way too big for Pumpkin anyway."

"I can see that," the woman said, smiling. "My name is Lydia Scoop, and I'm a reporter for the *Gazette*. First thing, I'd like to get a picture of Pumpkin for the paper. Can you bring her here for a photograph? Then I'll interview you all. If we can get this done today, I'll have the story ready for the paper tomorrow."

Amelia Bedelia looked at her friends. They all looked back at her and grinned.

Pumpkin was going to be famous—and so were they!

"We'll be right back!" said Amelia Bedelia.

"Mom! I'm home!" called Amelia Bedelia when she, Skip, Penny, and Joy rushed through the front door. "Guess what?"

"What?" her mother called. She came from the kitchen, carrying a tissue in one hand and her phone in the other. "Sweetie! You look like the cat that swallowed the canary!"

"Oh, no! Did Pumpkin eat a canary? She really likes birds. But, wait, we don't have a canary. And you said no more pets except

canary

for Finally. Did you change your mind?" Amelia Bedelia gasped in horror. "Did you get a canary today when I was at school? And did Pumpkin eat it already?"

"There is no canary," her mother said, pausing to blow her nose.

"Mom, guess what! A reporter named Lydia Scoop wants to do a story for the *Gazette* about Pumpkin!" said Amelia Bedelia. "We're supposed to take Pumpkin to the newspaper office so she can take her picture."

Amelia Bedelia's mother smiled. "That's wonderful. And I have good news, too. Lieutenant Johnson from the fire station just called and said that she's talked to all the other firefighters, and they've agreed that they want a cat to be their station pet. They'd like to adopt Pumpkin."

Amelia Bedelia and her friends cheered. "We did it!" shouted Joy.

"Our posters worked!" yelled Skip.

"Let's go tell Pumpkin!" Penny hollered.

Chapter 11

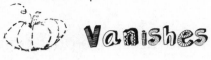 Vanishes

Clummmmp! Clummmmppp! Clumppppppp!
Chlump! Chlump!

All four kids raced up the stairs and burst into Amelia Bedelia's room. They sounded like a herd of buffalo.

"Guess what, Pumpkin? You've got a new home!" Amelia Bedelia shouted.

But there was no answer from

Pumpkin—not a single purr or meow.

Pumpkin was not rubbing against their ankles, begging for attention. She was not curled up on the pile of clean, folded laundry on Amelia Bedelia's bed. She was not batting the ears or chewing on the noses of Amelia Bedelia's stuffed animals.

They checked every corner of the room. They looked under the

bed and behind the dresser.
They searched the closet.
Finally they had to admit it—
Pumpkin was not there.

"Mom!" yelled Amelia Bedelia. "Did
you let Pumpkin out?"

"No, cupcake," answered her mother.
She came upstairs. "I haven't opened the
door of your room all day, except to put
the clean laundry on your bed."

Amelia Bedelia, Penny, Joy, and Skip
looked at each other.

"I bet Pumpkin snuck out when your
mom brought the laundry in," said Penny.
"My cats are really good at sneaking out
like that."

"Pumpkin must be somewhere else in

the house," said Amelia Bedelia.

"Please find her!" said Amelia Bedelia's mother. She sneezed three times.

Amelia Bedelia and her friends split up to search the house. But Pumpkin was not stretched out on the couch in the living room . . . or trying to poke her nose into the kitchen cupboards . . . or lurking under the dining table. She was not hiding in the bathtub or snoozing in the coat closet. Pumpkin had vanished.

Finally kept whining at the back door, scratching to go out. "Hey, girl, you

could help us search for Pumpkin, you know," said Amelia Bedelia, patting Finally on the head. "But go outside first." When she opened the door, Finally shot out into the yard with a joyful bark.

Amelia Bedelia saw a flash of orange and black and white dive into the hedge that separated their yard from the neighbor's.

"Pumpkin is outside!" she shouted to her friends. "Come on!"

The four friends raced into the yard. Amelia Bedelia pointed to the hedge where Pumpkin had vanished, and they all ran to the neighbor's yard. But by the time they got there, Pumpkin was nowhere to be seen.

"Oh, no!" wailed Penny. "This is utterly cataclysmic!"

"It sure is," agreed Amelia Bedelia. "But we'll find her. We need supplies."

Amelia Bedelia hurried back to her house and told her mother where she and her friends were going. She grabbed a container of tuna fish out of the refrigerator and Finally's leash from the hall closet.

"Finally loves Pumpkin," she told her mother. "I bet she can find her."

They looked under bushes and up in the trees. They searched flower beds and recycling bins. But there was no sign of Pumpkin.

"Here, kitty, kitty, kitty!" Amelia Bedelia

called. She held a morsel of tuna in front of her and waved it around.

They hurried down the sidewalk, stopping everyone they ran into. "Have you seen a lost cat?" they asked, over and over. "Black and orange and white."

But no one had seen Pumpkin.

Penny began to look worried. "What if she goes out in the street?" she asked anxiously. "And gets hit by a car? Or meets a mean dog? She probably thinks all dogs are as friendly as Finally, but some of them don't like cats. What if we can't find her at all?"

"We'll find her, Penny," said Amelia Bedelia. "We found her once. We can do it again."

Suddenly, Finally started to prance and wag her tail. She stuck her nose up in the air and sniffed.

"Look!" said Amelia Bedelia. "I bet Finally can smell Pumpkin!"

Finally definitely smelled something. She pulled hard on her leash, towing Amelia Bedelia in the direction of Oak Tree Elementary.

But Finally wasn't headed to the front entrance of the school. Or the playground. Instead she pulled them around the outside of the playground. Along one side of the street was the playground, and on the other side of the fence was the tree where they'd first found Pumpkin. Across

the street were the backyards of many different houses.

Finally dragged Amelia Bedelia to a gate that led into one backyard. Finally put her nose to the space where the gate met the ground and sniffed hard.

"Look, there's a hole where she's sniffing," said Joy, pointing.

It was a hole about the size of a young, small cat.

Finally whined and pawed at the hole. Pretty soon she'd dug a hole the size of an excited small dog.

"Finally, no!" said Amelia Bedelia, pulling her back. "Come on!" she said to her friends. "Maybe Pumpkin is in there!"

Amelia Bedelia unlatched the gate. She hoped that the people who lived there would not mind four kids and a dog barging into their backyard. After all, this was a genuine emergency.

The backyard had tomato plants and a big patch of mint around a stone patio with a picnic table. But it had no orange and black and white cat anywhere that the four friends could see.

Still, Finally was so excited that she danced up on her hind legs, spun in a circle,

and yanked her leash right out of Amelia Bedelia's hand. She raced up to an open window, barked, then sat with her nose in the air, sniffing as hard as she could.

Something was cooling on the windowsill. It was a pie with a crispy brown crust. It smelled of cinnamon and nutmeg and something else. Pumpkin!

Finally had led them to pumpkin, just as Amelia Bedelia had known she would— but not Pumpkin the cat. She had led them to pumpkin the pie!

Chapter 12

". . . but Satisfaction Brought Her Back."

Amelia Bedelia looked at Skip, Joy, and Penny in dismay. She'd been so sure that Finally would lead them to the right place. But it hadn't worked. Instead of finding a cat, they'd lost lots of time. By now Pumpkin might have wandered far away. How would they ever find her?

The patio door slid open.

"Hello? Hello?" said the woman who had opened it. She had curly white hair and glasses and smudges of flour on her purple sweater. "Can I help you? Are you looking for something?"

Amelia Bedelia nodded. "I'm sorry we came into your yard without permission," she said. "We're looking for a lost cat. We thought she was back here, but she's not."

"Oh, dear," said the woman. "What a shame. I'm so sorry. I lost a cat myself not long ago, and I know how worried you must be. But my cat came home this afternoon. Such a surprise! Maybe your cat will do the same thing. Would you like a piece of pumpkin pie before you go on looking?"

"Yes!" said Skip.

"We should keep searching," said Joy. "We need to find her."

"We'll have more energy after pumpkin pie," said Skip. His stomach growled.

"Amelia Bedelia, what do you think?" asked Penny.

The pie smelled very good indeed.

"Maybe just a teeny-weeny slice," said Amelia Bedelia.

Amelia Bedelia and her friends sat down at the picnic table while the woman, whose name was Mrs. Larkin, went inside. She came out again in a moment, carrying the pumpkin pie in one hand and a stack of paper plates in the other.

Two cats came outside with her, circling her legs and meowing as if they were begging for a bite of pie. "Cinnamon and Nutmeg, you silly girls!" said Mrs. Larkin. "This pie is not for you!"

Both cats were black and white and orange. One of them spotted Finally and backed away with her ears down. The

other trotted right over to Finally and touched her nose to Finally's nose. Then she rubbed her face against Finally's cheek and purred.

"It's Pumpkin!" yelled Amelia Bedelia.

Pumpkin jumped right into Amelia Bedelia's lap. She purred some more and nuzzled her head under Amelia Bedelia's chin.

"Is this the cat you were looking for?" asked Mrs. Larkin.

Amelia Bedelia and her friends laughed and explained everything—how they'd found Pumpkin in a tree in the corner of their playground, how the fire

purrrr

department had rescued her, how they'd been looking for a home for her ever since. Now a reporter from the newspaper wanted to write a story about her. But she'd gotten lost, until Finally had finally led them right to her.

"What a story!" said Mrs. Larkin. "What an adventure!"

"And it has a happy ending," said Penny. She reached out to pet Pumpkin—or Cinnamon—who was snuggled in Amelia Bedelia's arms.

"We tried so hard to find a home for her," said Skip. "And it turns out she found home for herself."

"A perfect home—her own home!" said Joy.

"Pumpkin—I mean Cinnamon—definitely thinks it's *purr*fect," said Amelia Bedelia. "Listen to her!" Then she opened her eyes wide. "But what about Lieutenant Johnson? She wants Pumpkin—I mean Cinnamon—to be the fire station cat!"

They explained to Mrs. Larkin how Lieutenant Johnson, who had rescued Cinnamon from the tree, now wanted to adopt her.

"Well, my goodness. That certainly puts the cat among the pigeons!" said Mrs. Larkin.

Amelia Bedelia held Pumpkin tight. "Somebody

pick up Nutmeg!" she said. "And hold on to Finally's leash!"

"I'm so happy to have Cinnamon back. I can't possibly give her away," said Mrs. Larkin. "But I do feel bad for that nice firefighter. What a pickle! What a problem! What should we do?"

Amelia Bedelia had an idea.

The next day, Amelia Bedelia's parents drove her to the animal shelter where they had adopted Finally. Slowly and carefully she looked at all the cats that were available. One was smoky gray . . . one was soot black . . . and one was fiery orange.

"That one," said Amelia Bedelia. "That's the right one!"

Amelia Bedelia and her parents explained the situation to the volunteers at the shelter. Amelia Bedelia promised to bring Lieutenant Johnson back to the shelter to meet everyone. Then she gave the animal shelter all the money that the class had raised for an ad in the paper, and they gave her the orange kitten. She sat in the back seat of the car and snuggled the cat on her lap as her parents drove her to the fire station.

Mrs. Larkin was already there, and she'd brought Cinnamon with her. So was Lydia Scoop from the newspaper. So was Mrs. Shauk. And Mr. Jack. So were Skip, Joy, Penny, Angel, Dawn, Cliff, Wade, Clay, and all the other kids from Mrs. Shauk's class.

"Lieutenant Johnson," said Amelia Bedelia. "We're sorry that you can't adopt Pumpkin—I mean Cinnamon—after all. But we think this cat is perfect for the fire station, and she needs a home. Will you adopt her instead?"

Lieutenant Johnson nodded as the

other firefighters cheered.

"You bet!" Lieutenant Johnson said, and she reached out and took the orange cat from Amelia Bedelia's arms. "She'll be the perfect fire station cat, and I think Pumpkin is the perfect name for her. You kids really are the cat's pajamas!" She looked at Amelia Bedelia's long, fleecy pants and soft, fuzzy shirt. She blinked. "Wait a minute. Are you wearing . . ."

Amelia Bedelia laughed. "Yep!" she said. "My cat pajamas!"

"Picture time!" called out Lydia Scoop.

They gathered around Lieutenant Johnson. Lieutenant Johnson held up the fire station's brand-new cat, and Lydia Scoop raised her camera high.

Everybody smiled. Even Cinnamon and Pumpkin and Finally looked as though they were smiling. But Amelia Bedelia, standing between Mrs. Larkin and Lieutenant Johnson with all her friends, had the widest smile of all.

Meee-oooo-wwww!
Cat Facts!

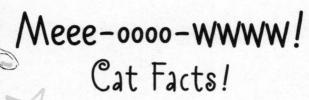

"Bezoar" is the official word for a hairball. BLECH!

There are more than 500 million pet cats in the world. That's a lot of cats!

Clowder = a group of cats

clowder

Kindle

Kindle = a litter of kittens

Tom = a male cat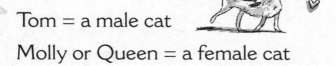

Molly or Queen = a female cat

The cat's meow? Meee-ooow!

Cats only meow at humans!

Because their claws go in one direction and their back legs are stronger than their front legs, cats are very good at climbing up trees but very bad at climbing down. Backing down the trunk is their best bet.

Meee-ooo-wwww!

MEEEEEOOOOOOOOOOOWWWWWWWW!

Did you know that in 1963, French scientists launched a cat named Félicette into space? She returned safely to Earth by parachute.

calico cat

One in every 3000 calico cats born is a male!

purrrrr

Meet Amelia Bedelia

The 10 best things about Amelia Bedelia:

1. She's very funny
2. She's brave
3. She's a good friend
4. She loves to read
5. She'll try anything
6. She makes really good cookies
7. She takes things literally
8. She never gives up
9. She loves her family
10. She always helps out

Two Ways to Say It

By Amelia Bedelia

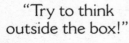

"Try to think
outside the box!"

"Try to think up
something new
and different."

"She sure thinks
on her feet."

"She can react quickly
to a new situation."

"Don't forget, curiosity
killed the cat!"

"Your curiosity
can get you into
dangerous situations."

"Cat got your tongue?"

"Why aren't you talking?"

"I'm a scaredy-cat."

"I'm frightened."

"It's like herding cats!"

"It's hard to organize something uncontrollable."

"You're a copycat!"

"You're doing the same thing I'm doing."

"She let the cat out of the bag."

"She told your secret."

"We want to see if you're worth your salt."

"We want to see if you're worth what we'll pay you."

"You're the cat's pajamas."

"You're great."

The Amelia Bedelia Chapter Books

With Amelia Bedelia, anything can happen!

Amelia Bedelia wants a new bike—a brand-new, shiny, beautiful, fast bike. A bike like that is really expensive and will cost an arm and a leg!

Amelia Bedelia is getting a puppy—a sweet, adorable, loyal, friendly puppy!

Have you read them all?

Amelia Bedelia is hitting the road. Where is she going? It's a surprise!

Amelia Bedelia is going to build a zoo in her backyard. Better yet, she is going to invite all her friends to bring their pets and help plan the exhibits and rides.

5

Amelia Bedelia usually loves recess, but one day she doesn't get picked for a team and she begins to have second thoughts about sports.

6

Amelia Bedelia and her friends are determined to find a cool clubhouse for their new club.

142

Amelia Bedelia is so excited to be spending her vacation at the beach! But one night, she sees her cousin sneaking out the window. Where is he going?

New steps inspire Amelia Bedelia and her dance school classmates to dance up a storm!

What does Amelia Bedelia want to be when she grows up? Turns out, the sky's the limit!

When disaster strikes and threatens to ruin her aunt's wedding, it's up to Amelia Bedelia to make sure Aunt Mary and Bob tie the knot!

An overnight camp is not Amelia Bedelia's idea of fun—especially not *this* camp, which sounds as though it's super boring and rustic. What Amelia Bedelia needs is a new plan, fast!

Amelia Bedelia and her parents are heading to the shore for summer vacation and that means sailing, surfing, eating a ton of ice cream, and just hanging out. And what about the mystery of the buried treasure?

Introducing...
Amelia Bedelia
& FRIENDS

Amelia Bedelia +
Good Friends =
Super Fun Stories
to Read and Share

Amelia Bedelia and her friends celebrate their school's birthday.

Amelia Bedelia and her friends discover a stray kitten on the playground!

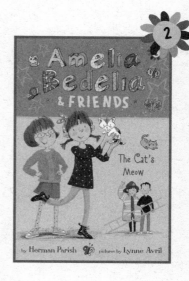

Amelia Bedelia and her friends take a school trip to the Middle Ages that is as different as knight and day.

Coming soon . . .

Spot the difference

These two pages are not exactly the same.
Eight things from page 148 are missing from
page 149. Can you spot them?